MY DAUGHTER, MY SON, THE EAGLE, THE DOVE

AN AZTEC CHANT

▲ ▲ ▲

▼ ▼ ▼

by **Ana Castillo**

illustrated by **S. Guevara**

DUTTON BOOKS *New York*

MY DAUGHTER,

THE DOVE

My daughter,
precious
as a golden necklace,

precious
as a quetzal plume,

you are my blood,
my image—

Now you have awoken;
you are of the age of reason.
Listen!

So that you may understand
the ways of this world.
Listen!

It is important
that you know well
how to live,
how to walk your path.

Look, my dear daughter,
my little dove—

The path is not
just a little hard,
it is frighteningly so.

Oh my daughter,
in this world
of such pain
and sadness

there is cold,
there are jarring winds,

heat that tires us,
that brings us hunger,
thirst.

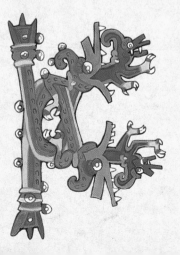

The gods have given us
laughter,
sleep,
food,
drink,

so that the bad
does not bring too much sadness,
does not always make us cry.

Understand, my daughter,
that you are of noble
and generous blood;

you are precious
as an emerald,

precious
as sapphire.

You were sculpted
of relations
cultivated like jade.

Do not dishonor yourself;
do not bring yourself shame,

nor to your ancestors
who were noble and good.

You have left your toys,
childhood games.

You understand now,
you are of the age of reason.

Don't be lazy.
Rise,
sweep—
Salute the gods!

Dress quickly,
wash your face,
hands,
mouth.
Keep yourself clean
always.

Listen!
My beloved daughter,
my dove,
my own:

Here is your mother
from whose womb you came

like a stone cut
from another

and who gave you life
as a plant gives life
to another.

I must teach you
what you should know

to live well
as you were meant.

When we are gone,
and you are on your own,
people will whisper
that we did well by you.

When we are gone
you will live honorably
among the dignified.

You were not meant
to sell herbs
at the market,
wood,
green chilies,
or saltpeter
on street corners.

You are noble!
My daughter,

note well and listen to
what I must tell you:

When you speak, speak
not too loud
and not soft

but with honest words
always.
Walk—

never with bowed head,
nor
ever raised too high.

Don't listen to gossip.
Don't repeat what is said
along the path.

Daughter of mine,
our ancestors, noblewomen,
ancient and white-haired,
told us these few words:

Listen!
Take heed!

In this world we go along
a narrow path,

very high
and very dangerous
below.

Do not stray.
Do not let yourself
fall.

Stay on the path.
Oh my daughter,
so tenderly loved—

Don't choose your life companion
like an ear of corn,
only for its golden color.

Choose your life companion with care.
You must live
all your days together.

And if you both be poor,
don't belittle your companion.

Have faith in the gods
who are all-merciful.

Be skillful,
understand,

learn what is Toltec,
what is noble.

Watch with diligence,
curiosity,
alertness

how to weave,
how to apply colors.

My daughter,
my turtledove,

this I have told you
so that you will always
know your worth.

Your heart is
a sapphire,
simple and clean.

Listen,
take note
of these things.
May they be your torch,
your firebrand
to guide you
throughout all your days
on this earth.

And with this, my duty is done.

May the gods give you a long
and happy life,
my beloved one!

MY SON,

THE EAGLE, THE TIGER

My son,
eagle, ocelot,
wing, tail,
so dear,
so beloved—
listen!

It is right
that you should take care.

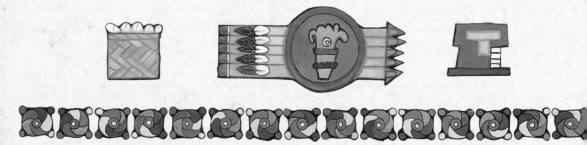

Listen!
Understand!
This is the place of hardships.

The old ones
of white hair and wrinkled faces,

our ancestors
have left it said for us:

They did not come
to be greedy,
to be restless.

Through their deeds,
they came to be known
as eagles,
as tigers.

Cut wood!
Plant the maguey:
you will have to drink, eat,
wear clothes.

You will be real.
You will walk the path.

By this work
you will be known,
by your parents
and relations.

Do not give yourself
too soon
to a companion—

tho' you be lonely,
filled with desire—

until you are grown
and have learned
to give.

The maguey
yields nothing
when still green.

When you find a companion—
what will you both eat, drink?
Will you suck air perhaps?

You are the support.
You must stand straight.

You are the eagle!
You are the tiger!

You will be praised
for your acts.
Not with envy

nor torn heart
will you speak,
but with honesty

and a good song
by which you will
be esteemed.

Listen and take note:
look wisely,
with good judgment
at things.

Although you be poor,
although your mother and father
were the poorest of the poor,
keep your heart pure,
keep your heart clean and real,
keep your heart firm.

Be alert!
Be swift
on your path!

Be calm and honest
in your ways.

You were not meant
to roam the mountains,
gathering weeds
to eat,
wood
to sell.

Carry yourself
well.

Do not be the
object of scorn
and ridicule.

Do not waste the days
and nights
the gods have given you.

Do not waste your body
with bad food,
bad habits,
a bad life—

You'll soon
die
a waste!

My son
so beloved:
listen to these words
and put them
in your heart.

They were left to us
by our ancestors,

the wise old men
and old women
who lived here
on this earth.

Keep these words
like gold in a coffer.

They are like emeralds,
jade,
sapphires,
resplendent and polished.

They are wide and fine
quetzal plumes
suited for nobility,

for those who live well
and are of good heart.

May the gods
who are near and far
and know all secrets,
see all things,
watch over you always.

May you be blessed
with peace.

With this my duty is done.
My greatest treasure,
my son, my beloved one.

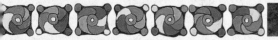

AUTHOR'S NOTE

In the land of what is now known as Mexico, the land of my ancestors, before the Conquest, from generation to generation the *huehuehtlatolli*, the ancient word, was spoken. The *huehuehtlatolli* were the teachings of the elders or the words of the wise, spoken here as a rite of passage by a mother, father, or schoolteacher. These rites of passage took place throughout a person's life from birth to death. The *huehuehtlatolli* was meant to affirm, support, and instruct the individual on the significance of the event and the responsibility that the individual had at that moment, such as during childbirth or going to war or, as in the case of the *huehuehtlatolli* excerpts here, coming of age.

My ancestors, the Mexica, known to most of the world as the Aztecs, were not a simple people at the time of the Conquest. Theirs was no longer an oral tradition. Instead, the wisdom of their own forebears, mainly the Toltecs, was written on *amate*, a kind of paper made from the bark of a fig tree. Written in hieroglyphics and in red and black ink (these colors together signified wisdom), the messages were—according to the Spanish friars from which we have our principal understanding of these words—thorough and effective. The learned chronicler Friar Bartolomé de las Casas said of the *huehuehtlatolli* that he had not known better lessons from Socrates, Plato, or Aristotle. Except that the Aztec gods to which the ancient words paid homage were replaced by the Christian God, the *huehuehtlatolli* were translated rather faithfully into Castilian by the friars in Mexico in the sixteenth century.

The *huehuehtlatolli*, metaphorically thought of as mirrors held before the disciple, were repeated over and over until the lessons were engraved in the person's heart and would serve as lifetime guides. The *huehuehtlatolli* were preserved for centuries. Times changed, but not so very much. People, less so.

The lessons in these excerpts apply as much to our children today as they did to the indigenous children of Mesoamerica hundreds of years ago. There are no new values or morals to teach the young. We have only to remember the basic ones that have held all complex societies together, the most basic of which are self-respect and respect for all other living things. There are drugs now. There were drugs and the temptation for abuse then. There are teen pregnancies now. The young women of Aztec society were also warned not to be careless about their bodies or to have sex before they were prepared to be mothers. There were unexplainable disease and war in that region as there are in the world now. The

young then were as inclined to disobey their elders as they frequently are today. That is why it was the duty of not just one adult in a young person's life, but of all adults, to instruct with love, care, and also by example and the firm conviction of one's beliefs.

As a mother and former teacher, I have found the *huehuehtlatolli* to be immensely inspiring and moving. I share here a few excerpts from the ancient teachings of my ancestors with the hope that they will also touch you and your loved ones.

And with this, my duty is done.

May your life be a long and happy one!

Ana Castillo

ILLUSTRATOR'S NOTE

My challenge with Ana Castillo's chant was to create a visual response. For inspiration, I immersed myself in research about Aztec daily life. I learned that the Mexica used extended metaphors both in writing and speaking to describe their relationship to their world and their gods. They did not have a writing system in the strict sense of the word. Instead, they used glyphs (symbols, figures, and geometric shapes) to describe concepts, people, and objects. Words were pictures, and pictures were words. This "picture writing" filled fan-folded books of bark or deerskin, which are referred to as codices. Very few of them remain in existence today.

It is difficult for historians to understand the exact meaning of these glyphs. What *is* understood is that the ancient codices were written/drawn in a style that prompted the reader to recall what was formerly only the oral story. The facing direction and scale of the glyphs—even the thickness of the line and color delineating them—created a visual landscape of metaphor and meaning for the storyteller. With a layperson's fascination, I researched and assigned meaning to certain glyphs as they appear in Mexica art. I integrated these glyphs into the contemporary story I painted on the *amate* (Mexican bark) paper.

Following the text, I divided my contemporary picture narrative into two parts—the daughter's story and the son's story. In the daughter's pictures, I tell the story of the birth of a baby girl (a dove) who grows up loving books. She later becomes a pediatrician. She marries a young man who is an artist and a teacher. They have a baby of their own. In the son's pictures, I tell the story of a baby boy (an eagle) born to a family that works the land. He knows he is an artist from an early age. He graduates from college and marries a young woman who is a pediatrician. A baby girl (a dove) is born to them, and the cycle of family begins anew. It is one story told first from one point of view, then the other. In this way, I sought to join the text about the boy and the girl and emphasize the circle of life.

Additionally, the glyphs create a metaphorical story. As in the post-Hispanic codices, I have placed name glyphs above the heads of the bearers. I chose a star glyph for the boy because his art is like light to the night sky. On page 38, I have painted a tiger upholding a red and black sky. As an art teacher, the son (who is the "tiger" of the chant) teaches a student (another tiger) how to paint. He gives the student the tools to be a wise tiger who can create art, which is like light to the night sky. The butterfly glyph for the girl symbolizes her importance and her connection to the earth. In the codices, fans carried by messengers denote an imperial mission and sometimes appear to connote healing. In the girl's visual imagery, the fan represents her mission to bring hope and healing, while the boy's fan represents his mission as an artist to reflect the world around him. My visual representations of these glyphs follow.

Star (name glyph for son)   *tiger*   *Butterfly (name glyph for daughter)*   *fan*

The flat glyph images of traditional Aztec figures outside the bark paintings illuminate the chant in a more direct way. They were taken directly from the *Codex Mendoza*, a post-Hispanic account of early-sixteenth-century Aztec life. The red and deep blue bars throughout refer to the Aztec idiom "red ink, black ink," symbolizing wisdom. Day sign glyphs (a circle within a circle) are connected to these bars and increase from page to page to reflect a lunar cycle and show roughly the length of a woman's menstrual cycle. They refer to fertility and our connection to the earth.

I encourage anyone interested in learning more about this magnificent language of picture writing to refer to the books listed below to achieve a fuller understanding of the background of Ms. Castillo's powerful chant and my visual representation of it.

The Essential Codex Mendoza. Frances F. Berdan and Patricia Rieff Anawalt, editors. Berkeley and Los Angeles: University of California Press, 1997.
The Codex Borgia. Gisele Diaz and Alan Rodgers, editors. New York: Dover Publications, 1993.
The Aztecs. Richard F. Townsend. London: Thames and Hudson, 1992.
Painting the Conquest. Serge Guzinski; translated by Deke Dusinberre. Paris: UNESCO: Flammarion, 1992.

I am not a master of the ancient glyph writing or of its interpretation, but I hope this book will give you, the reader, something evocative, poetic, and meaningful. I offer it to you to celebrate *your* eagles and doves.

S. Guevara

To mi'jito, Marcel Ramón,
and to the next seven generations

A.C.

For my eagle and my doves,
Liam, Rebecca, Megan, and Pamela

S.G.

SOURCES FOR THE CHANTS
Historia general de las cosas de Nueva España by Friar Bernardino de Sahagún. Editorial Nueva España, S.A., California 197–. Churubusco, México, D.F., 1946. Excerpts from Book XI, Chapters 17, 20, 21.
La filosofía Náhuatl by Miguel León-Portilla. Universidad Nacional Autónoma de México, Instituto de Investigaciones Historicas, México 20, D.F., 1974. Excerpts from early Nahuatl sources.
Huehuehtlatolli: Testimonios de la antigua palabra by León-Portilla and Silvia Galeana. Secretaría de Educación Pública, Fondo de Cultura Económica, México, 1991.

The anatomical figures used in conjunction with the borders were modeled on figures in the *Codex Mendoza*, a post-Hispanic pictorial and textual account of sixteenth-century Aztec life. More about this book can be found in *The Essential Codex Mendoza* by Frances F. Berdan and Patricia Rieff Anawalt, editors. University of California Press, Berkeley and Los Angeles, 1997.

CIP Data is available.

Published in the United States 2000 by Dutton Children's Books,
a division of Penguin Putnam Books for Young Readers
345 Hudson Street, New York, New York 10014
http://www.penguinputnam.com/yreaders/index.htm

Designed by Amy Berniker
Printed in Hong Kong
First Edition
10 9 8 7 6 5 4 3 2 1
ISBN 0-525-45856-5